Elliot
Bakes a Cake

For Trevor and Florence, who both love to bake!

Kids Can Press acknowledges the financial support of the Ontario Arts Council, the Canada Council for the Arts and the Department of Cultural Heritage.

Published in Canada by
Kids Can Press Ltd.
29 Birch Avenue
Toronto, ON M4V 1E2

Published in the U.S. by
Kids Can Press Ltd.
85 River Rock Drive, Suite 202
Buffalo, NY 14207

The artwork in this book was rendered in pencil crayon.
Text is set in Minion.

Edited by Debbie Rogosin
Designed by Karen Powers
Printed in Hong Kong by Book Art Inc., Toronto

CM 99 0 9 8 7 6 5 4 3 2 1

Canadian Cataloguing in Publication Data

Beck, Andrea, 1956–
    Elliot bakes a cake

"An Elliot Moose story".
ISBN 1-55074-443-7

I. Title.

PS8553.E2948E44 1999   jC813'.54   C99-930072-5
PZ7.B42El 1999

Kids Can Press is a Nelvana company.

Elliot
Bakes a Cake

Written and Illustrated by

Andrea Beck

Kids Can Press

ELLIOT MOOSE

was bursting with excitement. Today was a very special day.
He raced around the corner to find his friend Socks.
"It's Lionel's birthday," said Elliot. "Let's bake a cake!"
"A cake!" cried Socks. "That's a great idea!"

While Socks got ready,
Elliot hurried upstairs.
Amy and Paisley would
want to help, too.
"It's Lionel's birthday," he called. "Let's bake a cake!"
"Oh yes!" said Amy. "Lionel needs a cake."
"Oh boy!" cried Paisley. "We get to bake!"

Elliot, Amy and Paisley ran down to the kitchen.
Socks rushed in behind them.

Together, they told Beaverton their plan.

"Brilliant!" said Beaverton.

He dug through his cupboard and pulled out a card.
"Look!" he said, "I have just the recipe."

They quickly found everything they needed. Then Beaverton began to read the directions.

"First, we separate the eggs," he said.

"Separate the eggs?" asked Elliot. "What does that mean?"

"It's easy!" laughed Socks.

She got two teacups and put an egg into each one.

Elliot was surprised. Didn't eggs have to be cracked open?

"Now, cream the butter,"
read Beaverton.

"Cream the butter?" asked Elliot.
"How do we do that?"

"Simple!" said Paisley.

He dropped a big square of butter
into a bowl and poured in some cream. But when he
stirred, they wouldn't mix together.

Beaverton frowned. "Try adding the sugar,"
he suggested.

It was Amy's turn. She added the sugar and
stirred round and round.

"Look!" yelled Socks. "It's mixing!"

Elliot smiled. Now they were getting somewhere.

"Next, we beat the eggs," said Beaverton.

"Beat the eggs?" repeated Elliot. "What does *that* mean?"

Nobody knew. So Elliot cracked open the eggs and stirred them into the big bowl. He mixed and mixed and mixed.

"It's starting to look like batter," declared Socks.

Elliot wasn't so sure. It looked lumpy.

Wasn't batter supposed to be smooth?

"Time to add the milk and flour," announced Beaverton.

In went the milk. In went the flour.

Then Beaverton added a spoonful of baking powder. "So our cake will be nice and tall," he said.

They took turns stirring until most of the lumps were gone.

"It looks like proper batter now," said Paisley.

"I think you're right," agreed Beaverton.

Elliot and Socks poured the batter into a pan and placed it gently in the oven.

Everyone gathered to watch the cake bake.

"How will we know when it's done?" asked Elliot.

Beaverton checked his recipe. "When we touch the middle of the cake it will spring up," he said.

"It will spring up?" Elliot was amazed.

He stared eagerly through the oven window, looking for the first hint of movement.

After a short while, Beaverton opened the oven and Elliot touched the cake. But it didn't spring up. It wobbled.

The next time they checked the cake, it looked just right. But when Elliot touched the middle, it didn't spring up. It didn't even quiver.

They put it back in the oven and began to make the icing.

When they were finished, they checked the cake again. It *still* didn't spring up. It didn't jump up. It just sat there.

"This cake's not planning to move at all," declared Elliot. "And it's looking awfully dark."

Socks peered over Elliot's shoulder.

"Oh no!" she wailed.

Elliot's heart sank. He looked at Socks.

Lionel's cake was burnt!

The kitchen was silent.
Everyone stared at the cake.
It wasn't just a little burnt. It was *very* burnt.
Elliot struggled to hold back his tears.
There would be no birthday cake for Lionel.

After a few unhappy
minutes, Elliot brightened.
"We can fix it!" he said.

Bit by bit, he cut off the outside of the cake.

"Isn't it getting awfully small?" asked Socks.

"Yes, but with the burnt parts off, at least it
will taste good."

Next, Elliot cut the little cake into three layers.
Amy spread jam on two, and Paisley covered the
top with icing.

"It looks great!" said Elliot. "But a birthday cake should be extra special."

They got back to work and decorated the cake.

When they were done, it was the most beautiful cake they had ever seen.

At last they were ready to surprise Lionel.

The five friends carried their cake up the stairs, one careful step at a time.

They were so excited that it was hard not to giggle.

"Shhh!" whispered Elliot. "He'll hear us!"

But Lionel was reading. He didn't suspect a thing.

"HAPPY BIRTHDAY, LIONEL!"

"My stars!" gasped Lionel. "What a beautiful cake!"

They all crowded around while Lionel made his wish, blew out the candles, and served the cake.

There was just enough to give everyone a tiny piece.

"Mmmm," said Lionel. "This is the best cake I have ever tasted."

Everyone agreed.

It was the best cake they had ever tasted.

A Very Special Cake

Mix together in a separate bowl:
2 1/4 c. (575 mL) all-purpose flour
3 1/2 tsp. (17 mL) baking powder
1/2 tsp. (3 mL) salt

2 eggs
3/4 c. (175 mL) soft butter
1 1/2 c. (375 mL) sugar
1 c. (250 mL) milk
1 tsp. (5 mL) vanilla

First, separate the eggs into two small bowls. Next, in a big bowl, cream the butter. Now, add the sugar. Stir until smooth. Beat the egg yolks, then mix them with the butter and sugar. Add the milk and vanilla and stir. Add the flour, baking powder and salt a little at a time. Mix until smooth. Beat the egg whites until they are stiff, then gently fold them into the batter. Pour the batter into two greased 9-in. (1.5-L) pans and spread evenly. Bake in a preheated oven at 350°F (180°C) for 30 minutes or until the centers spring up when touched.

Always ask an adult to
help you use the oven.